Los Secretos de Abuelo Sapo

Keiko Kasza

Traduccón de Cristina Aparicio

GRUPO
EDITORIAL

norma

http://www.norma.com
Barcelona, Bogotá, Buenos Aires, Caracas, Guatemala, Lima, México, Miami, Panamá,
Quito, San José, San Juan, San Salvador, Santiago de Chile.

Para Kimihiro y Rika

Un agradecimieto especial para mi esposo, Greg,
que siempre lee mis manuscritos
con ojos de especialista y con corazón de niño.

Kasza, Keiko
    Los secretos del Abuelo Sapo / Keiko Kasza. – Bogotá:
Grupo Editorial Norma, 2006.
    32 p. : il ; 27 cm. – (Buenas Noches)
    ISBN 958-04-9399-5
    1. Cuentos infantiles japoneses 2. Animales - Cuentos infantiles
3. Fábulas japonesas I. Tít. II. Serie.
I895.65 cd 19 ed.
A1080536

    CEP-Banco de la República-Biblioteca Luis Ángel Arango

Título original en inglés:
Grandpa Toad's Secrets

Una publicación realizada por G.P. Putnam's Sons, acuerdo con
una división de The Putnam and Grosset Group.
Copyright © 1995 del texto original en inglés e ilustraciones por Keiko Kasza.

Copyright © 2006 para Hispanoamérica por Editorial Norma S.A.
A.A. 53550, Bogotá, Colombia.
Impreso por Editora Géminis Ltda.
Impreso en Colombia — Printed in Colombia
Enero de 2010

ISBN 958-04-9399-5
ISBN 978 -958-04-9399-0
C.C. 11566

Un día Abuelo Sapo y Sapito
salieron a caminar por el bosque.

—Sabes, Sapito —dijo Abuelo—, nuestro mundo está lleno de enemigos hambrientos.

—¿Cómo nos podemos proteger, Abuelo? —preguntó Sapito.

—Bueno —declaró Abuelo—, voy a compartir mis secretos contigo. Mi primer secreto es ser valiente. Debes ser valiente al enfrentarte con un enemigo peligroso.

En ese preciso momento apareció una culebra.

—Hola, sapos —siseó la culebra—. ¡Me los voy a comer de almuerzo!

Sapito dio un alarido y corrió a esconderse. Pero, ¿Abuelo estaba asustado?

¡Ni un poquito!

—¡Cómeme si puedes! —gritó
ferozmente Abuelo—. Quizá yo soy mucho
más grande de lo que tú puedes tragar.

Abuelo tomó aire y se hizo cada vez más
y más grande.

—Pues... tal vez otro día —murmuró la
culebra y se fue lentamente.

Sapito saltó de los arbustos.

—¡Oh, Abuelo! —gritó—. ¡Fuiste tan valiente! ¡Estuviste maravilloso!

Abuelo Sapo sonrió lleno de alegría.

—Gracias —le dijo—. Pero algunos enemigos son demasiado grandes para espantarlos. Mi segundo secreto es ser astuto. Debes ser astuto al enfrentarte con un enemigo peligroso.

En ese preciso momento apareció una gran tortuga voraz.

—Hola, sapos —chasqueó la tortuga—. ¡Me los voy a comer de un bocado! *¡Chas, chas!*

Sapito dio un alarido y corrió a esconderse. Pero, ¿Abuelo estaba asustado?

¡Ni un poquito!

—¿Un bocado? —preguntó Abuelo—. ¿No prefieres un banquete?

—Claro que sí —respondió la tortuga.

—Hace poco una apetitosa culebra pasó por acá. Si te apresuras la puedes atrapar.

—Gracias por el consejo —dijo la tortuga y se fue muy rápido a cazar a la culebra.

Sapito saltó de los arbustos.

—¡Oh, Abuelo! —gritó—. ¡Fuiste tan astuto! ¡Estuviste maravilloso!

Abuelo Sapo sonrió lleno de alegría.

—Gracias —le dijo—. Ahora, el tercer y último secreto.

Pero antes de que pudiera decir otra palabra...

Un enorme monstruo apareció.

—Hola, sapos —rugió el monstruo—. ¡Me los voy a comer sólo por diversión!

Sapito dio un alarido y corrió a esconderse. Pero, ¿Abuelo estaba asustado?

¡Sí! ¡Estaba asustado!
Nunca en su vida había visto
una criatura más espantosa.
Intentó escapar, pero el
monstruo lo atrapó.

Sapito estaba escondido entre los arbustos temblando de miedo. Pero recordó los secretos de su abuelo:

¡Ser valiente y astuto!
¡Ser valiente y astuto!

Vio unas bayas silvestres y decidió rápidamente lo que debía hacer.

Sapito le lanzó las bayas al monstruo.
Las bayas se reventaron y le dejaron manchas
rojas en las patas. El monstruo ni siquiera se dio
cuenta. ¡Estaba muy ocupado convirtiendo a
Abuelo en un sándwich de sapo!

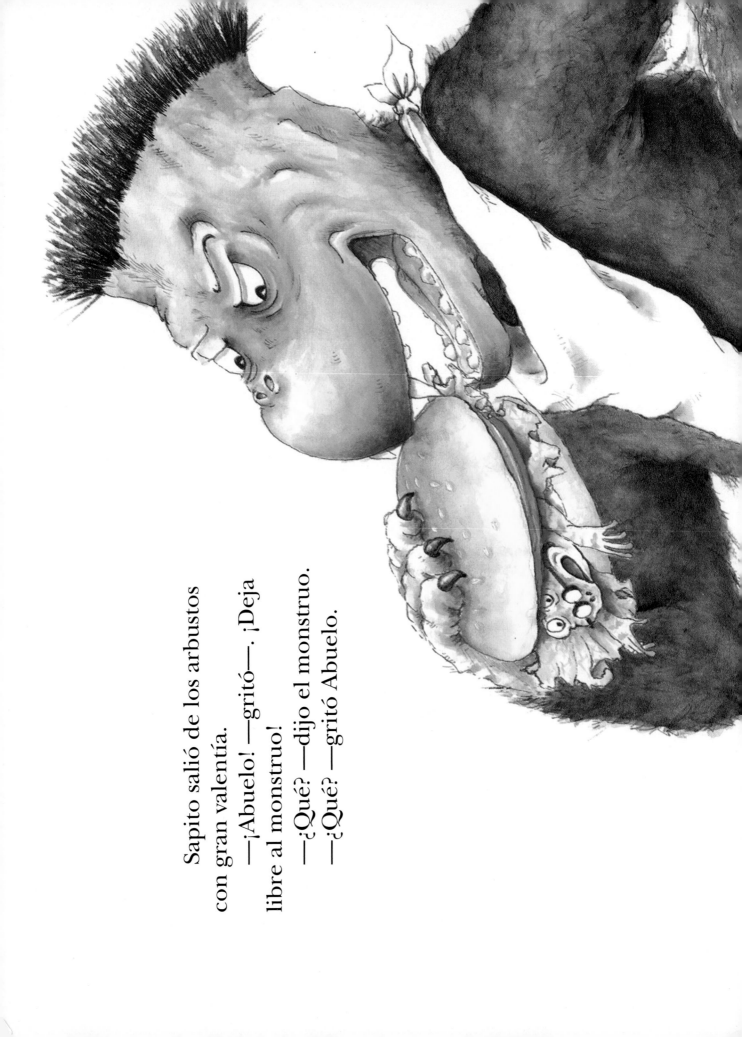

Sapito salió de los arbustos con gran valentía.

—¡Abuelo! —gritó—. ¡Deja libre al monstruo!

—¿Qué? —dijo el monstruo.

—¿Qué? —gritó Abuelo.

—Abuelo —dijo Sapito—, no es muy amable de tu parte andar por ahí envenenando monstruos. Tu veneno ya le está subiendo por las patas. Pronto tendrá manchas por toda la cola y luego morirá. ¿No te da vergüenza, Abuelo? El monstruo se miró las patas.

—¡Socorro! ¡Socorro! ¡Estos sapos malvados me están envenenando!

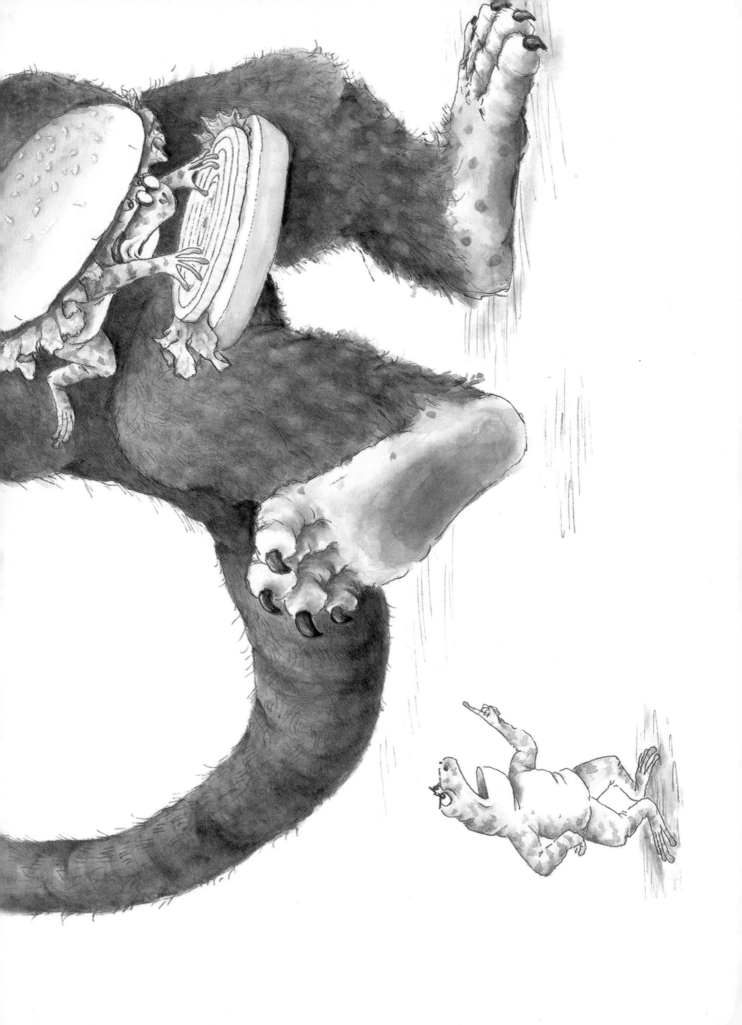

El monstruo corrió tan rápido como pudo. Abuelo y Sapito se abrazaron.

—¡Uf! —suspiró Abuelo—. Estuve cerca.

—Sí —dijo Sapito.

—Bueno —dijo finalmente Abuelo—, pero aún no has escuchado mi tercer secreto.

—¿Cuál es? —preguntó Sapito.

—Mi tercer secreto es éste —declaró
Abuelo—: en caso de emergencia, estar
seguro de tener un amigo con quien contar.
Sapito, fuiste tan valiente. Fuiste tan astuto.
¡Estuviste maravilloso!

Esta vez fue Sapito quien sonrió lleno
de alegría.

Racecars: Start your Engines!

Molly Aloian and Bobbie Kalman

Crabtree Publishing Company

www.crabtreebooks.com

Created by Bobbie Kalman

Dedicated by Andrew Elliott
For everybody who hears the sound of a race car flying by and dreams of winning the Indy 500

Editor-in-Chief
Bobbie Kalman

Writing team
Molly Aloian
Bobbie Kalman

Substantive editor
Kathryn Smithyman

Editors
Kelley MacAullay
Michael Hodge

Photo research
Crystal Foxton

Design
Margaret Amy Salter

Production coordinator
Heather Fitzpatrick

Prepress technician
Nancy Johnson

Consultant
Petrina Gentile Zucco, Automotive Journalist, The Globe and Mail

Special thanks to
North American Solar Challenge;
Panasonic World Solar Challenge and Events South Australia

Illustrations
Vanessa Parson-Robbs: back cover, pages 8, 10, 32 (Formula One cars)
Margaret Amy Salter: pages 7, 18, 23, 32 (all except Formula One cars)

Photographs
Dreamstime.com: © Shariff Che'lah: pages 16-17; © Elemér Sági: page 25;
   © Tomislav Stajduhar: page 32 (rally cars)
Icon SMI: David Allio: page 23; Brian Cleary: page 21; Vincent Curutchet/DPPI:
   page 24; Gilles Levent/DPPI: front cover, page 11
iStockphoto.com: Nicola Gavin: page 32 (go-carts); Tan Kian Khoon: pages 1, 5;
   Stefan Klein: page 10; Jason Lugo: page 20; Jacom Stephens: pages 4, 26-27
Stefano Paltera/North American Solar Challenge: page 28
Image courtesy of Panasonic World Solar Challenge and Events South Australia:
   pages 29, 32 (solar cars)
Cody Images/Photo Researchers, Inc.: pages 30, 31
© ShutterStock.com: Todd Taulman: page 18; Derek Yegan: page 22
Other images by Corel

Library and Archives Canada Cataloguing in Publication

Aloian, Molly
   Racecars : start your engines! / Molly Aloian & Bobbie Kalman.

(Vehicles on the move)
Includes index.
ISBN 978-0-7787-3043-9 (bound)
ISBN 978-0-7787-3057-6 (pbk.)

   1. Automobiles, Racing--Juvenile literature. I. Kalman, Bobbie, 1947-
II. Title. III. Series.

TL236.A46 2007   j629.228   C2007-901068-7

Library of Congress Cataloging-in-Publication Data

Aloian, Molly.
   Racecars : start your engines! / Molly Aloian and Bobbie Kalman.
      p. cm. -- (Vehicles on the move)
   Includes index.
   ISBN-13: 978-0-7787-3043-9 (rlb)
   ISBN-10: 0-7787-3043-3 (rlb)
   ISBN-13: 978-0-7787-3057-6 (pb)
   ISBN-10: 0-7787-3057-3 (pb)
   1. Automobiles, Racing--Juvenile literature. I. Kalman, Bobbie.
II. Title. III. Series.
   TL236.A3945 2007
   629.228--dc22
                                          2007005690

Crabtree Publishing Company

www.crabtreebooks.com   1-800-387-7650
Copyright © **2007 CRABTREE PUBLISHING COMPANY.** All rights reserved. No part of this publication may be reproduced, stored in a retrieval system or be transmitted in any form or by any means, electronic, mechanical, photocopying, recording, or otherwise, without the prior written permission of Crabtree Publishing Company. In Canada: We acknowledge the financial support of the Government of Canada through the Book Publishing Industry Development Program (BPIDP) for our publishing activities.

Published in Canada
Crabtree Publishing
616 Welland Ave.
St. Catharines, ON
L2M 5V6

Published in the United States
Crabtree Publishing
PMB16A
350 Fifth Ave., Suite 3308
New York, NY 10118

Published in the United Kingdom
Crabtree Publishing
White Cross Mills
High Town, Lancaster
LA1 4XS

Published in Australia
Crabtree Publishing
386 Mt. Alexander Rd.
Ascot Vale (Melbourne)
VIC 3032

Contents

What is a racecar?

A **racecar** is a **vehicle**. A vehicle is a machine that moves from place to place. Racecars often have bright colors. This racecar is bright red.

Racecars are made to move very fast!

Driving in races

People drive racecars in **races**.
Races are contests. They are contests
to see which car and **driver** can go the
fastest. A driver is a person who drives
a racecar.

There are many kinds of races. There are also many kinds of racecars. Keep reading to learn more about these fast vehicles!

Powerful parts

Racecars have many parts. Each part does a different job. One of the most important parts is the **engine**. The engine gives the racecar **power**. Power makes the racecar move.

Some racecars have **wings**. Turn to page 9 to read more about wings.

A racecar has **wheels**. There are **tires** on the wheels. The tires are made of rubber.

The driver uses **brakes** to make the car slow down and stop.

Some racecars have only one seat. Other racecars have two or more seats.

The driver wears a **helmet** on his head.

A racecar has a **cockpit**. The driver's seat is in the cockpit.

The driver uses the **steering wheel** to steer the car.

Sleek and smooth

The shape of a racecar is very important. A racecar has a sleek, smooth shape. Having a sleek, smooth shape helps a racecar move quickly.

A racecar is low to the ground. Being low to the ground helps air flow over the racecar. When air flows over the racecar, the racecar can move faster.

Wings down

Wings help a racecar move quickly. As the racecar moves, air flows over the wings. The air pushes down on the wings. The air pushes the car down, too. When the racecar is pushed down, the tires are pressed to the ground. A racecar drives fastest when its tires are pressed to the ground.

There is a wing at the front and at the back of this racecar.

Race courses

Racecars race on **courses**. A course is an area for races. Each course has a starting line. It also has a finish line. Some courses are **tracks**. Tracks are wide paths. Most tracks have oval shapes.

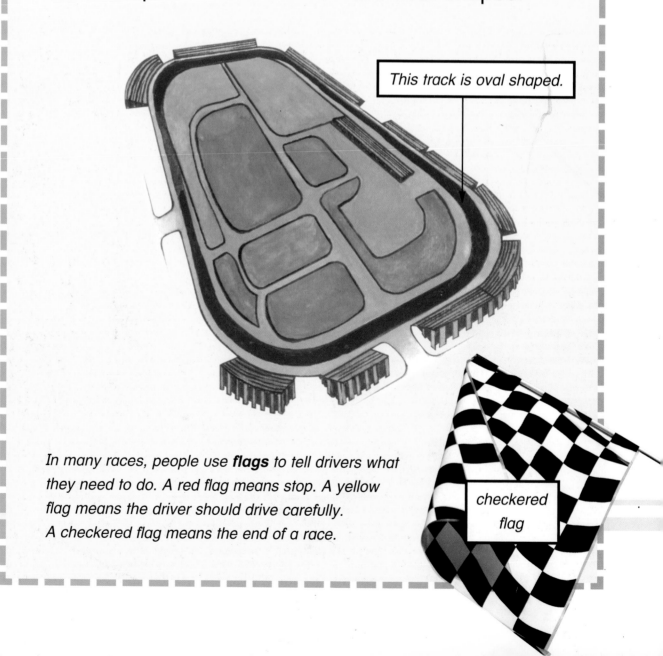

This track is oval shaped.

In many races, people use **flags** to tell drivers what they need to do. A red flag means stop. A yellow flag means the driver should drive carefully. A checkered flag means the end of a race.

checkered flag

Road courses

Some courses are **road courses**. Road courses are on roads and streets. The roads and streets are in cities and towns. During a race, only racecars can drive on road courses. The roads and streets are blocked off. No other cars or people can go on them.

Sports cars

Some racecars are **sports cars**. There are many kinds of sports cars. Porsches and Corvettes are two kinds of sports cars. Sports cars are built for racing. Sports cars race on oval tracks. They also race on road courses.

This racecar is a Ferrari. A Ferrari is another kind of sports car.

Short or long?

Some sports car races are short. The cars drive around the course only a few times. Other races are hundreds of miles long. During long races, the sports cars speed around the course many times.

Pit stops

Racecars cannot finish long races without stopping. Racecars need to stop for **fuel**. Gas is a kind of fuel. Engines need fuel to make power. Racecars stop in areas at the sides of the courses. The areas are called **pits**.

This racecar is stopped in a pit.

Quick checks

A stop in a pit is called a **pit stop**. During a pit stop, **mechanics** pump fuel into the racecar. Mechanics are people who check and fix machines. The mechanics also change the tires on the racecar.

The mechanics work very quickly. They can change all four tires in seconds! They work quickly so the racecar can begin racing again.

Formula One cars

Formula One cars are the fastest kind of racecars. They race mainly on road courses. Formula One races are called Grand Prix races. There are different kinds of Grand Prix races.

*A Formula One car is an **open-wheel car**. An open-wheel car has wheels on the outside of the car. An open-wheel car is built for racing.*

An open-wheel car has only one seat.

Stick to the formula!

People build Formula One cars using a **formula**. A formula is a set of rules. Formula One cars are all the same length. They are all the same weight. The engines of Formula One cars are all the same size, too.

Indy 500 cars

Indy 500 cars are open-wheel cars, just as Formula One cars are. Indy 500 cars are longer and heavier than Formula One cars are, however. Indy 500 cars race on oval tracks.

Indianapolis 500

Many cities have tracks on which Indy 500 cars race. One track is the **Indianapolis Motor Speedway**. The main race for Indy 500 cars is held on this track. The race is called the Indianapolis 500. The racecars travel 500 miles (805 km) during the Indianapolis 500.

Indy 500 cars can zip around tracks faster than at 200 miles per hour (322 km per hour). This speed is more than twice as fast as a regular car can go!

Stock cars

A **stock car** looks a lot like a regular car that you see on roads. All the parts in a stock car are built for racing, however. A stock car has a very big engine. The engine is powerful. The tires on a stock car are smooth. They are called **slicks**.

The smooth slicks on this stock car help the car grip the track.

NASCAR

The National Association for Stock Car Auto Racing (NASCAR) holds races for stock cars. Most NASCAR races are on tracks. NASCAR races are exciting to watch! Many cars race around the track at once. The cars are very close to one another. It is hard for the drivers to get ahead of the other cars.

Dragsters

A **dragster** is built for speed. It is built to reach **top speed** in just a few seconds! Top speed is the fastest speed that a vehicle can go. Dragsters race in races called **drag races**.

Dragsters do not race around oval tracks like other racecars do. Dragsters race on short, straight tracks. Often, only two cars race against each other at a time.

Using parachutes

A dragster is racing at top speed when it reaches the finish line. It moves so fast that it needs help stopping. Some dragsters have **parachutes**. A parachute is a large circle of cloth. It shoots out at the back of the racecar. The parachute helps the dragster stop.

Right on rallies!

Rally cars are tough racecars. They are built to race long distances in races called **rallies**. Rallies are not held on tracks or road courses. The courses may be partly on roads, but they are also on mud, rocks, and grass. Rallies take place in all kinds of weather. Rally cars sometimes drive through rain, snow, and on ice.

This rally car is taking a flying leap over a bump.

All fours

Rally cars must be able to drive over bumps. They steer through slippery mud. Many rally cars have **four-wheel drive**. With four-wheel drive, all four wheels get power from the engine at the same time. Cars with four-wheel drive are good at driving over slippery or rough ground.

Rallies are long races. They take several days to finish.

Go-carts

Go-carts are the smallest racecars. They are light and very low to the ground. Go-carts have small wheels and engines. Having small wheels and engines makes go-carts slower than other racecars. Drivers race go-carts on short tracks.

Many famous racecar drivers learned how to race in go-carts.

Solar cars

Solar cars are different than other racecars. Their engines are not like the engines of other racecars. Solar cars get power from sunlight. Sunlight gives these racecars the power to move. Solar cars cannot go as fast as other racecars can.

Solar cars look different than other racecars do. They are wider, flatter, and lighter than other racecars are. Being wide and flat helps solar cars get as much sunlight as possible.

A very long race

The World Solar Challenge is a race for solar cars. The race takes place in Australia, where it is very sunny. The solar cars race a long way! They race all the way across Australia. The race takes many days to finish.

This solar car has just started the World Solar Challenge in Australia.

A super-fast car

The **Thrust SSC** is the fastest car on Earth! SSC stands for **supersonic car**. A supersonic car can go faster than the speed of sound. The Thrust SSC has two engines. The engines are **jet engines**. Jet engines are the same engines as the engines in jet airplanes. Having jet engines makes the car go very fast.

The Thrust SSC is the most powerful car on Earth!

Breaking the record

In 1997, a man named Andy Green drove the Thrust SSC in a desert in Nevada. He drove it for 19 miles (31 km). During the drive, he drove faster than any other driver has ever driven. Andy Green drove the Thrust SSC 763 miles per hour (1228 km per hour)!

Words to know and Index

dragsters
pages 22-23

Formula One cars
pages 16-17, 18

go-carts
pages 26-27

Indy 500 cars
pages 18-19

solar cars
pages 28-29

sports cars
pages 12-13

rally cars
pages 24-25

stock cars
pages 20-21

Thrust SSC
pages 30-31

Other index words

Printed in the USA